ABDO

A FAMILY OF EDUCATIONAL PUBLISHERS

IMPRINT: Leveled Readers

NEW SERIES: World of Reading Level 1 Set 5

TITLE: Doc McStuffins: Starry, Starry Night

LIBRARY BOUND ISBN: 9781532141874

EBOOK ISBN: -

MULTI-USER EBOOK ISBN: -

READ-TO-ME EBOOK ISBN: -

LIBRARY OF CONGRESS #: 2017961158

TRIM: 6.25" x 9.25"

LIBRARY BOUND PRICE: $ 17.95

ANYWHERE EBOOK PRICE: -

READ-TO-ME EBOOK PRICE: -

PAGES: 32 pp

READING LEVEL: Grade 1

RELEASE DATE: January 2019

Starry, Starry Night

Adapted by Bill Scollon
Based on the episode by Michael Rabb
Based on the series created by Chris Nee
Illustrated by Character Building Studio and the Disney Storybook Art Team

ABDOBOOKS.COM

Reinforced library bound edition published in 2019 by Spotlight, a division of ABDO, PO Box 398166, Minneapolis, Minnesota 55439. Spotlight produces high-quality reinforced library bound editions for schools and libraries. Published by agreement with Disney Press, an imprint of Disney Book Group.

Printed in the United States of America, North Mankato, Minnesota.
092018   012019

 **DISNEP PRESS**
New York • Los Angeles

THIS BOOK CONTAINS
RECYCLED MATERIALS

Library of Congress Control Number: 2017961158

Publisher's Cataloging-in-Publication Data

Names: Scollon, Bill, author. | Rabb, Michael, author. | Character Building Studio; Disney Storybook Art Team, illustrators.
Title: Doc McStuffins: Starry, starry night / by Bill Scollon and Michael Rabb; illustrated by Character Building Studio and Disney Storybook Art Team.
Description: Minneapolis, MN : Spotlight, 2019 | Series: World of reading level 1
Summary: Doc's friend, Henry, brings his telescope to Doc's house to watch a meteor shower. But before it begins, Henry discovers his telescope isn't working. Can Doc fix it?
Identifiers: ISBN 9781532141874 (lib. bdg.)
Subjects: LCSH: Doc McStuffins (Television program)--Juvenile fiction. | Telescopes--Juvenile fiction. | Toys--Juvenile fiction. | Meteor showers--Juvenile fiction. | Readers (Primary)--Juvenile fiction.
Classification: DDC [E]--dc23

Spotlight
A Division of ABDO
abdobooks.com

Doc McStuffins is excited.
Her brother, Donny, is excited, too.

They are going to watch a
meteor shower!

Doc tells Donny about meteors.
"Meteors are glowing rocks that
race across the sky."

Dad made star-shaped cookies.
"The cookies are star-tastic!"
Doc says.

Henry lives next door.
He has a new telescope.

Doc wants to see it. Hurry, Doc!
The meteor shower starts soon.

Henry shows Doc the telescope.
Oh, no! Everything looks blurry.

The telescope is broken.
Now Henry will not see the meteors.

Doc wants to fix the telescope.
Hurry, Doc! The meteor shower
starts soon.

Henry will wait with Donny.
"I'll be right back," says Doc.

The Doc is in!
Doc's toys come to life.

They say hello to the telescope.
Her name is Aurora.

Aurora cannot see well.
She thinks Lambie is a dog!

Doc knows what to do.

"Time for your checkup!" says Doc.

Doc shows Aurora a picture
of a whale.

Aurora thinks the whale
is a pretzel.

Doc knows what is wrong.
"Aurora has Blurry-star-itis!"
she says.

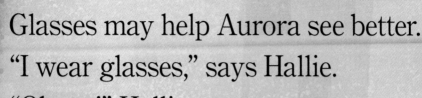

Glasses may help Aurora see better.
"I wear glasses," says Hallie.
"Oh, no!" Hallie says.
"My glasses are missing."

Hallie finds her glasses.
"Maybe Aurora is missing
something, too," Doc says.

Doc looks at Aurora's box.
Aurora is missing her eyepiece!

Aurora needs the eyepiece.
It will help her see well.

Doc thinks the eyepiece fell out.
It may be in Henry's yard.
"Road trip!" says Stuffy.

"Is the telescope fixed?" Henry asks.
"Almost," says Doc.

Hurry, Doc! The meteor shower
starts soon.

Doc looks for the eyepiece.
The eyepiece is in the grass.

Doc puts the eyepiece on Aurora.

Aurora looks at the sky.
She can see the stars.
She can see the moon.
The eyepiece works!

Doc gives Henry the telescope.

The telescope is fixed.

Thanks, Doc!

The meteor shower starts.
Meteors race across the sky.

Henry looks through his telescope.
He can see the meteors!

"How do you like the meteor
shower?" Dad asks.
"It is star-tastic!" says Doc.